BIG BIBLE
ADVENTURES

JACK'S GIANT PROBLEM

MARISSA PATTON

Illustrated By: LYNDA SLATTERY

TABLE OF CONTENTS

ACKNOWLEDGMENTS

I would like to acknowledge my dad for instilling in me from a young age the love for reading and writing! You are an inspiration to me!

Thank you to my mom for being a perfect picture of godly grace (pun intended).You are truly my inspiration for Mrs. Gracie.

To my son, Landon, your birth sparked a fire in me to work on and begin this book-writing endeavor. You have pushed me to be better than I ever could have imagined.

To Mrs. Renée Patton, thank you for your time and energy as you read my manuscript and gave me such great encouragement. Thank you for your faithful stand for the Lord.

To my heavenly Father, thank you for giving me the skills I have. Thank you for putting this vision in my heart and giving me the people and tools I need to see this come to pass! Thank you for salvation! Thank you for being my Father!

DEDICATION

I want to dedicate this book to my loving husband, Nate.
Thank you for making this dream possible for
me in so many ways! Your encouragement and
constant support have made this dream a reality.
I love you!

Character Introduction

JACK MORRIS - ready for adventure, pretty short

ORVILLE FERGUSON - enjoys research and reading, often gives nerdy facts and statistics

ALEX SHARP - twin to Allie, rides the bus to church, curious

ALLIE SHARP - twin to Alex, rides with the bus with her mom and brother, quite shy

CHLOE HART - loves frills and bows, outspoken and kind

MRS. GRACIE MIDDLETON - fourth grade Sunday school teacher, gentle and sweet, poised

DAVID - shepherd boy, fights Goliath

KING SAUL - king of Israel, strong solider, afraid to fight Goliath

GOLIATH - giant, enemy of God and the Israelite people

Chapter One

THE BIG BIBLE

"I am not short!"

Mrs. Gracie Middleton heard Jack Morris's voice as she walked down the hallway. She was a teacher for the fourth-grade Sunday school class.

When she got to the door, she saw her student Jack standing on a chair. Jack was

dressed up for church with a white shirt and tie. It looked liked he was trying to make himself taller than his classmates.

Orville Ferguson was standing nearby adjusting his round glasses. The rest of the class seemed to be enjoying the show. Each student turned in his seat for a better view. When Mrs. Gracie walked in, the class tried to hide their giggles.

"Jack, please get off of the chair," Mrs. Gracie said as she watched Jack grudgingly climb down from his perch.

"Orville said I was short!" Jack explained as he slumped in the chair.

"I said no such thing. I was simply trying to explain to Jack that he was, without a doubt, in a lower percentile for his age in connection with his height in comparison to others. I was speaking statistically, Jack, not out of spite."

Orville looked around the class to see if anyone else would agree with him. He did not recognize that what he said had hurt Jack's feelings.

Chloe Hart spoke up. "Yes, Mrs. Gracie! That is all Orville said. He is always talking about statistics and stuff no one else understands."

Mrs. Gracie could see that Orville did not mean to hurt Jack's feelings. She watched Jack hang his head. He was embarrassed. She thought for a moment, then knelt down in front of Jack and said softly, "Jack, do your friends at your school or other children you play with make fun of you for being short?"

"Sometimes," Jack mumbled. "I wish I were bigger."

Mrs. Gracie patted Jack's shoulder as walked to the front of the classroom. She noticed two new students in Sunday school this week. She looked at her student checklist and saw their names - Alex and Allie Sharp. They were twins and new riders on the church bus today.

"Good morning class! First, let us

welcome our two new guests. Alex and Allie, we are excited to have you in Sunday school today. I am Mrs. Gracie." She then turned and wrote on the white board with a marker - Psalms 118:8. "Do I have a volunteer to read this verse?"

Mrs. Gracie looked around the room for a student to raise their hand.

Chloe raised her hand high, waving it around. She opened her pink Bible, carefully turning to the verse. She stood and clearly read the words of the verse, "'It is better to trust in the Lord than to put confidence in men.'" She smoothed the ruffles in her flower dress as she took her seat again. She took a moment to adjust her curls and ribbon headband.

"Excuse me, Mrs. Gracie, but I do not understand the meaning of this verse." Orville squinted his eyes as if he were trying to figure out a difficult word problem.

"I think that I have a way to explain this verse to you, Orville, and help Jack feel better. Class, are you ready for your Sunday school lesson?" Mrs. Gracie had a mysterious gleam in her eye.

Alex shoved his hands in his jeans and rolled his eyes, "Oh brother, another boring Bible story I have to listen to."

Alex had been to other churches before. He did not like Sunday school very much. Alex and Allie's mom had ridden the bus too and insisted that they ride with her. Allie seemed much more eager about the lesson than her brother Alex.

Chloe looked at Alex in shock. "This is not just another Bible lesson! Mrs. Gracie makes the Sunday school lesson the best part of our week! It is not really a lesson. It is an adventure! Right, Mrs. Gracie?"

"Girls." Alex rolled his eyes again. "Why are they always so dramatic?"

Allie playfully punched her brother's arm, "We would rather be dramatic than

boring like boys." She winked at Chloe. The two girls shared a giggled.

With that, Mrs. Gracie walked to the side wall near the white board. There against the wall stood a black leather book. It was as tall as the whole wall. It had the words "HOLY BIBLE" etched in tall gold letters.

"Jack, why don't you turn to I Samuel 17," Mrs. Gracie said as she unlatched the pages of the Big Bible.

Jack turned the large pages as he searched and found the correct passage. All of a sudden, the verses cleared the page. A picture appeared. The students could see a beautiful hillside of green grass covered with fluffy white sheep. Then the sound of the sheep's high "Baa" filled the classroom. Somewhere in the distance was a peaceful melody.

"Whoa!" The class all murmured with excitement. They were frozen, their jaws hanging in shock.

"What are you waiting for?" Mrs. Gracie asked as they still stood in amazement. "Let's go!" And she stepped right into the Big Bible's pages and onto the grassy hillside.

Chapter Two

THE BEAR ATTACK

The students stepped right into the Big Bible and looked around.

"Where are we?" Jack asked. The wind blew the grass even as the hot sun beat down on the children.

In the distance, Jack could hear the sheep's constant bleating. *I think I hear singing*, he thought as he looked around for the source of the music.

Orville studied his surroundings. "We seem to be in a Middle Eastern country, if I am not mistaken. It is quite hot for this time of year." He squinted up at the sun.

"Hey! What happened to my jeans? And my T-shirt?" Alex looked down at his new outfit.

All of the students' clothes had been changed to biblical robes and sandals.

"Ah!" Orville adjusted his glasses. "Our garments have been changed to represent the historical time in which we have traveled. I would estimate approximately 900 B.C. Am I correct, Mrs. Gracie?"

Mrs. Gracie just laughed as she watched her students take in their new outfits and surroundings.

Chloe twirled with Allie as they admired their flowing robes, complete with colorful head pieces. The boys were not as excited as the girls to be in boyish tunics, but they were more comfortable than a church neck tie, so no one complained.

Mrs. Gracie announced, "You will get your church clothes back after our trip. Now listen, class." The group all stopped their chatter and listened.

"What do you hear?" Mrs. Gracie asked.

Music? Sure enough, the children could hear the soft stopping and starting of a

harp and what sounded like a boy's voice. The melody of the song was beautiful.

Before anyone could say anything, Chloe began running to discover the source of the song. Everyone followed close behind. As they reached the peak of the hill, a loud roar sounded from the edge of the field.

"Look out!" Jack hollered and pointed.

Out of nowhere came the biggest bear Jack had ever seen. Even the bear at the zoo last week was not this big! The creature leaped right toward the class!

Everyone began crying for help. They ran in every direction.

The bear was right behind Jack. Jack ran with all his might. The bear was gaining fast. Jack peaked over his shoulder as he ran. The bear was about to pounce! *I am a goner!* Jack squeezed his eyes shut, expecting the worst.

Just before the bear reached Jack, it stopped. Jack turned around to see that the bear suddenly toppled backwards into the thick grass. It kept toppling all the way down the steep hill.

Jack carefully peeked over the edge. The bear lay at the base of the hill. It was dead.

Jack gasped for air. He looked around for his new hero, "Thank you!" Jack huffed, "I thought I was about to be that bear's breakfast. How did you do that?"

"It was no problem! I used my sling. The rock hit the bear in the head. I am glad you are safe," said the young boy.

"Who are you?" Allie asked as the class slowly made their way up to the hilltop.

"My name is David. I am a shepherd. I have to protect my father's sheep from attacks just like this one all the time. Today, I helped protect you!"

David was so young and short. The class wondered how David could protect anyone.

Jack noticed that David seemed to be as short as he was. He guessed that David was just a bit older than him though. The shepherd boy wore sheep skin and a belt with a little bag on his side. He held a staff in one hand.

31

Allie gave David a shy smile. "I was so worried when I saw you running towards that bear! I am afraid of bears. May I see your sling?"

David held up his leather straps. "That bear wasn't too bad. Last week, I had to use my staff and my sling to protect the flock from a lion! But God always helps me do my job."

Chloe straightened her sash. "You were so brave! Do you sing too? We heard music earlier. I love music!"

David walked to the tree. He picked up a small harp. "This is mine. I use it to play and sing praises to God. I hope to write down my music and songs. One day maybe

others could sing the songs I write. But right now, I must be on my way! My father has sent me to take some food over to my brothers. They are fighting in the king's Israelite army."

"Yes! Now we will really see some action! Can we come with you?" Alex begged.

Allie shivered in fright. "I do not want to go to see any fighting! I am afraid of fighting."

Chloe patted Allie. "You cannot be afraid of everything, Allie. Don't worry. Mrs. Gracie would not let us go anywhere unsafe."

The class looked at Mrs. Gracie.

Mrs. Gracie nodded, "Of course we can go see David's brothers! But, class, I do not think that it is going to be the battle you are expecting."

Chapter Three

THE GIANT GOLIATH

Mrs. Gracie's class followed David to his home. His father gave him bread and cheese for his brothers. Soon, they were on their way to the battlefield.

"We are almost there," David pointed. "The battlefield is just over this rise."

But as they reached the peak, it seemed much too quiet for a battle.

"Whew! I thought this was going to be like the battlegrounds I've seen in my history book. This is as calm as a walk in the park!" Chloe and Allie looked relieved.

"Something is not right," David looked around. There were tents scattered about the hillside, but the camp seemed deserted. "Where are all the soldiers? Why isn't anyone fighting? Something must be wrong! I better go find my brothers."

The group took off running through the rows of tents. Jack noticed the soldiers' weapons lined the ground unused. They finally reached the edge of camp. All of the men were lined up along the top of a low valley. David spotted his brothers in the crowd and went to greet them.

"They must be getting ready to charge the enemy!" Alex whispered to Jack.

The boys nearly shook with excitement. *But how are they going to charge the enemy with their swords still in the camp?* Jack thought.

But instead of the noise of battle, Mrs. Gracie's students heard a booming voice from across the valley. The voice was awful. It was harsh and mean. It reminded Jack of one of the bully's he had encountered at school last week. The class pushed their way to the front of the soldiers. The voice was coming from the ridge across the valley.

"It's a giant!" Allie squeaked. She tried to hide behind Mrs. Gracie's skirt.

Allie was right. The man they saw was a giant. David and his friends listened as the terrible man bellowed across the valley.

"Choose a man to come and fight me! If your man kills me, then we will be your servants. But," the giant let out an evil laugh, "If I kill your chosen warrior, you will become our servants!"

The giant continued to mock the Israelite soldiers and even blasphemed God. Pretty soon, he and his army turned back to their camp.

"Who was that?" Chloe whispered up to Mrs. Gracie.

Mrs. Gracie answered, "That horrible man is Goliath. He is the champion fighter for the enemy-the Philistines."

Alex's face twisted in confusion, "The Philly steams?"

"No, Alex! The Philippines. It is a country in the Pacific Ocean made up of thousands of islands. It has a large population compared to its..." Orville stopped realizing that he may have made an error in his observation and looked at Mrs. Gracie for assistance. After all, Orville was not right all of the time.

Mrs. Gracie tried hard to hide her smile, "Philistines, Orville. Not the Philippines.

The Philistines are the greatest enemies of the Israelite army."

"Who is going to fight this giant?" David asked the three strong looking men standing next to him. *Those must be his brothers*, Jack thought.

"David, it's just a warrior from the Philistine army. He has come out for forty days now saying the same speech..."

"Forty days?!" David continued, his voice rising with anger. "He said some terrible things about God and the Israelite army. He is the enemy. He must be stopped!"

"Why are you here, David? You think you can fight this giant. You think you are more brave than the rest of us? Goliath

43

is the biggest man in the Philistine army. He is almost ten feet tall! And he has four brothers just as big as him! No one wants to fight against that." David's brothers towered over David. "You are too young and too small to be of any help. How can you possibly understand? Go back home to your sheep!"

"Is there not a cause? This is war! Everyone is just standing around. Someone has to fight him! He mocked the Lord and all of Israel!" Jack watched as David gave each word with more and more power. He wished he had the bravery of David.

"Listen, David, take your sling and your staff and go home. Go back to the fields

where you belong." His brothers turned and walked away. They did not even take the food David offered them from their father.

"Mrs. Gracie?" Chloe looked upset," "Why are David's brothers so angry? Why won't one of them fight Goliath?"

"Because they are cowards!" Alex exclaimed.

"They do not look ready for battle. That's for sure," Jack said.

David paced in front of the group. "There must be a way for someone to fight this giant."

Before anyone could answer, a young man came running into the camp calling for David.

"David, son of Jesse! Are you here?"

"I am David."

"I am a servant to King Saul. He wishes to speak with you at the palace. If you will just follow me, I will take you to him."

David nodded, "Can my friends come as well?"

"I am sorry. Only you were summoned. Follow me. We will return shortly."

"I will be back soon!" David waved at Mrs. Gracie and her class before following the servant out of the camp towards the city and the palace.

"Oh no, David is in big trouble now!" Allie whispered.

Jack became curious. Why would the king want to see David? How did the king even know that David was at the camp? Jack wanted to help David. Jack decided to sneak after David.

Jack looked around. When no one was watching, he grabbed a cloak from one of the tents. He used the cloak to cover his head and secretly took off after David. He hoped he would not get caught. No one saw him leave. Well, Mrs. Gracie saw him, but she knew that God had something for Jack to learn. She told no one of his secret escape.

Chapter Four

THE PALACE

Jack stayed close behind David and the servant. He dodged carts and horses in the city. He even walked past little vendors selling fruits and bread along the dusty street. Jack's stomach grumbled from hunger. *I cannot stop now*, he thought. *If I stop for a snack, I will lose them.*

Jack followed David around the corner and down a narrow alley. When he reached the end, he saw King Saul's palace. The palace was both beautiful and quite massive!

As he entered the gates, Jack had to duck behind the columns in the entry to keep from being seen. There were rows of soldiers guarding the hallways. Jack watched as David was led to a long throne room. At the end of the room sat King Saul on his throne.

David bowed before the king. Jack stood frozen in place behind the pillar. He did not want to give away his hiding place. He also did not want to miss one word.

"King Saul, you asked me to come to you. What is your request?" David said. His words echoed off of the marble walls.

"I have no request! Is what I have heard true? Do you intend to fight Goliath?" Saul looked unhappy.

It seemed to Jack that the king should be glad to find anyone willing to fight this evil Goliath. The greatest military fighters in the Israelite army did not want to fight him. And for the past forty days, not even this King went to challenge Goliath!

David answered with great respect, "I believe that God has brought me to the battlefield today to kill this unholy enemy of the most High."

"But you are too young David." Saul stood and began to pace the floor. "Goliath has been a fighter since he was a boy. He is much too big for you, David. You are still a boy yourself."

David replied with boldness, "King, I have kept my father's sheep for years. I have killed both a lion and a bear to protect those sheep. God was with me during those times. How can I not go and fight against this man? Goliath mocks the very God that has always been faithful to me. He seeks to destroy God's people. I cannot sit by and allow that to happen!"

Jack watched Saul turn to whisper to his servant. Soon, a suit of armor was brought out for David. The metal suit clattered together as the servants helped David put on each piece of armor.

"This is my very own armor. It is the best that is made. You will wear it to fight Goliath." King Saul was proud of himself.

Jack still wondered why King Saul did not fight Goliath. After all, King Saul was much taller and bigger than David. *Well, at least with armor, David will be protected*, Jack thought.

David almost collapsed under the weight of the heavy armor. The breastplate hung loose on his small frame and the helmet drooped low, almost covering his eyes.

"I cannot wear this, King Saul. It is much too big for me. I will fight with the weapons the Lord has given me- my sling and my staff." David began to take the protective armor off.

"NO!" Jack could not stay put any longer. He came running from his hiding place behind the column. "You can't fight Goliath! I won't let you!"

"Guards, grab that boy!" King Saul's voice bellowed as he stood and pointed in Jack's direction. The guards quickly obeyed. They snatched Jack up by his arms and began to carry him away. He kicked his legs wildly and fought to get free from the tight grip, but the guards would not budge.

"Jack? What are you doing here?" David came to Jack's rescue. "Your highness, this is a friend of mine. He must have followed me from the battlefield. Please, let him go."

As Jack freed his arms from the guards' hold, he exclaimed, "You cannot go against that giant with just your little sling and a stick! You'll be killed for sure! Please, David, won't you wear this armor?"

David put his arm around Jack's shoulder, "You know, Jack, you are short like me. But God has never lost a fight for me even though I am small. It is better to trust in the Lord than to put confidence in men. I have to trust Him to help me be strong and fight Goliath. Now, are you ready to head back to the battlefield? I know a giant that needs to be taught a lesson in respect."

Chapter Five

CONFIDENCE IN THE LORD

"Mrs. Gracie! Are you sure we will find Jack? He has been gone a long time!" Allie said in a sad voice.

Jack's classmates had looked all over the camp for him. They were beginning to get worried.

Mrs. Gracie smiled knowingly, "Jack will be back soon. Now stop worrying so much!"

Just as she said the words, Jack and David walked into camp. The soldiers hovered around David. They all wanted to know why he had to go see King Saul.

David said nothing. Instead, he started walking to the edge of the ridge and down toward the valley.

The whole class gathered around Jack.

"Where did you go? We were worried sick that you had been lost!" Chloe scolded.

Jack did not answer. Instead, he watched as David walked to the dried riverbed at the bottom. The class turned to watch too.

"What is he doing?" Alex looked at Mrs. Gracie.

Mrs. Gracie said, "He is gathering five smooth stones from the riverbed."

"But why? Jack, do you know what he is doing? Won't you tell us?" Chloe asked.

Jack swallowed hard and answered in a shaky voice. "David is going to fight Goliath."

As the children stood, they felt the ground shake beneath their feet. They looked across to the next ridge with wide eyes. There in the valley stood Goliath.

When Goliath saw David, he barked out a laugh. "Am I a dog? Is this the best that the God of Israel can do to fight against a champion like me? This is just a young boy!"

The class moved closer to get a better view. They crouched behind a boulder at the edge of camp. They each held their breath in wonder.

David then began to run towards Goliath as fast as he could.

"Why is he running towards him, Mrs. Gracie?" Allie covered her eyes.

"He is going to get killed for sure. I do not think you want me to tell you the statistics of this battle." Orville shook his head in despair.

"Go, David. Go!" Jack whispered a cheer.

"Allie, uncover your eyes," Mrs. Grace said as she patted Allie on the back, "You are not going to want to miss this."

David pulled one of the smooth stones from his shepherd's bag and placed it in his sling.

Jack and the class watched in amazement as David put the stone in his sling and began to swing it around and around.

Goliath charged forward, "Ahhhhh!"

David kept swinging his sling faster and faster and faster. Goliath raised his long spear. David kept swinging. Then, when the giant was close, David let his sling go! The stone went flying through the air. Mrs. Gracie's class gasped in shock.

THUMP! The stone hit Goliath right in the forehead. He stumbled back a bit.

Lord, please give David the victory to prove your power! Jack prayed silently.

Suddenly, Goliath crashed facedown into the dirt.

The Israelite army began to roar and cheer! Someone yelled, "Charge!" The Israelite army charged down across the valley, straight to the Philistine army. The Philistines turned and retreated in fear. Their champion was dead.

Mrs. Gracie's fourth grade Sunday school class clapped in victory!

"He did it! He defeated the giant!" Chloe jumped up and down.

"I can't believe it!" Jack said, "God really did help David!"

"And all he used was a rock!" Alex said.

"A stone to be precise," Orville corrected.

Mrs. Gracie led the rowdy class back to the camp.

"Look!" Chloe pointed to the edge of the tents.

Off in the distance, stood the Big Bible. The students saw their classroom through the pages. Jack's spirit fell a bit. He knew that he would never be as brave as David. If he left now, then he might never understand how David had killed the giant.

Just then, David ran up! "I thought you had left! I wanted to tell you all goodbye."

"It was very nice to meet you, David. Thank you for bringing us along through your amazing victory today." Mrs. Gracie smiled.

Jack looked at David, a new hero in Israel! David reached out and handed Jack his sling. "I want you to have this," he said. "Maybe it will remind you of what God can do in your life."

Jack took the sling and turned it over in his hands. He gave it back to David. "Nah! You keep it! I think God will be reminding me of this day for the rest of my life."

Each student waved goodbye to David then took their turn stepping through the pages of the Big Bible. Mrs. Gracie was the

last. She closed the Big Bible and fastened the latch to keep its pages safe until the next Sunday school adventure.

Alex looked around the classroom, "That was so much fun! Can we travel to another Bible story?"

"Well, every week for Sunday school, we get to see another story. But you know, there was a lesson to be learned in today's story." Mrs. Gracie searched the room for a volunteer.

Jack jumped up and down, "I know! David was young like us. He was even as short as I am!"

Orville agreed "Yes. And I find it quite a miracle that he was able to defeat both a lion and a bear, as well as the giant."

"Then, he saw someone who was going against God. Goliath even cursed God." Allie shook her head in disbelief.

"So what did David do to overcome the enemy? Is there anything he could have done differently?" Mrs. Gracie was enjoying her class's enthusiasm.

Chloe thought for a moment, "I guess he could have worn armor..."

"Nope! Wrong!" Said Jack, "Try again."

Mrs. Gracie smirked at Jack's obvious knowledge of the correct answer.

Chloe huffed, "Well, he was lucky he had his sling! David fought Goliath unprepared if you ask me."

Jack was not able to keep quiet anymore, "No, Chloe! He did not go unprepared. He planned to only take his sling and staff. Come on, guys! Don't you see? God gave him courage and strength. The king was going to give David his armor, but it didn't fit. Instead of asking for other armor, David told the king that God was going to fight for him." Jack stood and continued without taking a breath. He motioned with his hands to make his point more obvious to the class. "David told me that God had never let him down. He said he was going to use the sling and staff because that is what he used when protecting the sheep. Then, David had faith that God would take care of him, even though Goliath was much bigger than he was. This means that we can have faith in God too! Even when we feel small, or we are scared, or...." Jack stopped and took a breath. He looked around. The whole class was watching him. His cheeks turned red from embarrassment.

Mrs. Gracie gave Jack a resounding high five. "You are exactly right, Jack. We would all be wise to let God fight our battles. That is what our verse was about this morning. Psalms 118:8, 'It is better to trust in the Lord than to put confidence in men.'"

"Hey! That is what David told me at the palace!" Jack said.

"Well, David wrote the book of Psalms. I am sure he learned quickly that God is more powerful than any man could ever be, no matter his size."

Just then, the Sunday school bell rang. It was time for the class to join their parents in the sancutary for the church service.

"I hope you will all be in Sunday school next week!" Mrs. Gracie waved goodbye to each of her students.

As they filed out into the crowded hallway, the students promised to be at Sunday school that next week. Even Alex said he would be back.

Jack was the last to leave. "Thank you, Mrs. Gracie. I know now that no matter how small I am, I can still do big things for God, just like David."

THE END

CHALLENGE #1

1. WHAT DID YOU LEARN FROM JACK'S GIANT PROBLEM?

_____

_____

_____

_____

_____

_____

2. WHERE IN THE BIBLE IS THE STORY OF DAVID AND GOLIATH FOUND?

_____

3. DID DAVID DEFEAT GOLIATH?

_____

FIND THE CHARACTERS FROM THE STORY:

```
D D A O P I X E F H
I S R A E L I T E S
K I I C X A O U X D
G B V K F L Z G Y P
O V I I B L F T Z H
L O M N E I G Y N I
I R R G A E L B S L
A V S S R J A R H I
T I G A K Q L O J S
H L R U Q L E T A T
S L A L E H X H C I
M E C B B Y U E K N
I W I G X L B R S E
Y L E P Y P L S V S
H P C H L O E O P H
```

JACK

ALLIE

ALEX

CHLOE

ORVILLE

MRS. GRACIE

ISRAELITES

BROTHERS

GOLIATH

KING SAUL

PHILISTINES

VERSE #1
EPHESIANS 6:10
"FINALLY MY BRETHREN, BE STRONG
IN THE LORD, AND IN THE POWER
OF HIS MIGHT."

VERSE #2
PHILIPPIANS 4:13
"I CAN DO ALL THINGS THROUGH CHRIST
WHICH STRENGTHENETH ME."

VERSE #3
2 TIMOTHY 1:7
"FOR GOD HATH NOT GIVEN US THE SPIRIT
OF FEAR; BUT OF POWER, AND
OF LOVE, AND OF A SOUND MIND.

VERSE #4
2 CORINTHIANS 12:9
AND HE SAID UNTO ME, MY GRACE IS
SUFFICIENT FOR THEE: FOR MY STRENGTH
IS MADE PERFECT IN WEAKNESS. MOST
GLADLY THEREFORE WILL I RATHER GLORY
IN MY INFIRMITIES, THAT THE POWER OF
CHRIST MAY REST UPON ME.

About The Author

Marissa Shiflett Patton was saved at the age of six. At the time, she and her family were missionaries in South Africa. Marissa spent her childhood as a very happy missionary's kid.

When she was nine, her family moved to South Carolina were she was actively involved in church ministries and attended a Christian school. The summer before her senior year, her family moved to Maryland. After completing high school at Calvary Baptist School, she attended Bible college. There, she met her husband, Nathan Patton.

Nathan and Marissa are serving as missionaries in the Philippines. Marissa enjoys reading, writing, and being a mom to her son, Landon.

Made in the USA
Middletown, DE
23 June 2022

67570705R00050